THE
Littlest Candle
A HANUKKAH STORY

RABBIS KERRY & JESSE OLITZKY

Illustrated by Jen Kostman

Kalaniot Books
Moosic, Pennsylvania

nside a small house, inside a small drawer, lived a group of candles. One December evening, the candles peeked out of their drawer and shouted for joy. The sun was beginning to set. It was almost Hanukkah!

Chag sameach! Happy Hanukkah!" said Waxy, the wisest of the candles. "It's time for our favorite holiday. For eight nights our flames take center stage, and we get a chance to shine." All the candles began chattering.

"Now," Waxy added, "we have to decide which of us will be lit on the first night."

The candles jumped up and down. Each one raised a hand.
"Pick me," said Glow. "No! Pick me!" Twinkle yelled louder.
The candles pushed one another out of the way for the chance
to be chosen.

Little Flicker, the smallest of the candles, sat quietly listening from the corner. He didn't like to stand out and be the center of attention. He knew he could never compete with the taller candles. Even if he raised his hand, his wick wasn't high enough to be seen.

"Hanukkah celebrates the victory of the tiny Jewish army led by the Maccabees over the giant Assyrian-Greek army—a victory for the underdog," Waxy continued.

"When the Maccabees reclaimed the Temple in Jerusalem, they wanted to light the menorah that was inside. There was only enough oil for one day," Little Flicker added quietly. "But the menorah burned brightly for eight days. "

"That's right," Waxy said. "In olden days we used oil. Today, we usually light candles on this holiday to bring light into the world and to celebrate the miracle of the Maccabees. Hanukkah is a reminder that sometimes, even when you are small, you are still capable of miracles."
Flicker smiled from his place at the back of the drawer.

Waxy remembered how the small candle always volunteered to clean up the corners of the drawer where the larger candles couldn't reach. Little Flicker might be small, but he certainly had a big heart.

As the candles talked over each other, trying to prove that they were the best, Sparky and Sparkle took a step forward. The twins were always lit together every week to welcome in Shabbat and took their job very seriously.

Sparky always made sure to remember the time so that the candles were ready exactly at sunset on Friday. And Sparkle made sure to protect the peace during the ceremony so the calm of Shabbat could settle over all who celebrated. "We are the Shabbat candles," they said in unison. "Every week we are the first to welcome Shabbat on Friday night. We should also be the first to welcome Hanukkah."

"Great idea," Little Flicker called out from the back of the drawer. "They deserve it. They know how it's done!"

Smokey looked down at Little Flicker as the small candle spoke.

He remembered that Little Flicker often waited until all the other candles had eaten to be sure there was enough for everyone. First doesn't always mean best, thought Smokey.

"Don't be silly!" Ms. Wicks, the tall twisted candle, stepped forward. "I am the Havdalah candle," she said, trying to make her voice sound very important. "I am lit every Saturday night to end Shabbat. My strong, bright light helps carry the joy of Shabbat into the rest of the week."

She brushed back the wicks on her head as she continued. "My flames are so strong because I'm actually three braided candles. I am the strongest, so I should be the first candle lit in the menorah," Ms. Wicks demanded.

"The Havdalah candle makes a good point," Little Flicker agreed. "She's like all the flames of the menorah in one single candle. She is strong and would make a good choice."

"But sometimes that strength can be dangerous," thought Blaze.
He remembered the time Ms. Wicks's flames were so big they
almost got out of control. Little Flicker had alerted everyone to the
danger. Thank goodness for his quick thinking!

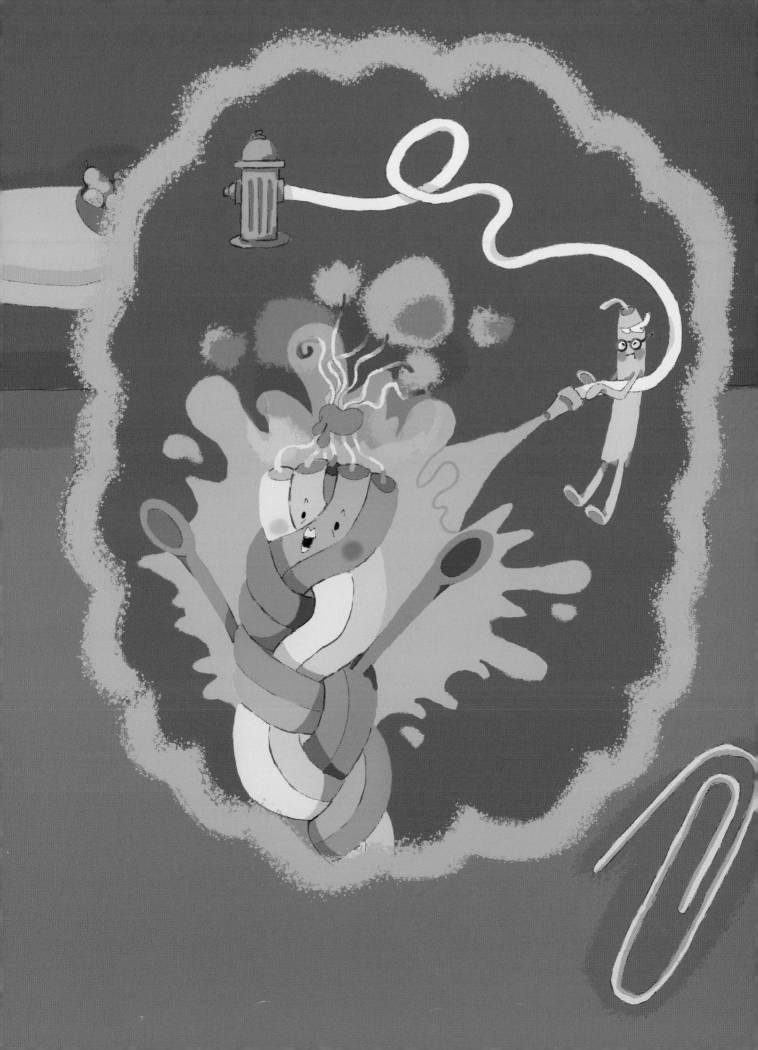

Waxy tried to restore order. "Listen up," he said. "If we cannot agree on a candle to be lit first, then maybe we should all be lit at the same time."

"But that's not how it's done," Little Flicker whispered. "We start with one candle and then add another candle each night, because the great rabbis have taught us that the light in the world should only grow brighter."

"That's true," Waxy said. "Who said that?" he asked, looking around at all the candles. Not a single one raised their wicks. "Who said that?" he asked again.

"It was me," Little Flicker said. All eyes turned to the back of the drawer to the tiny torch in the corner.

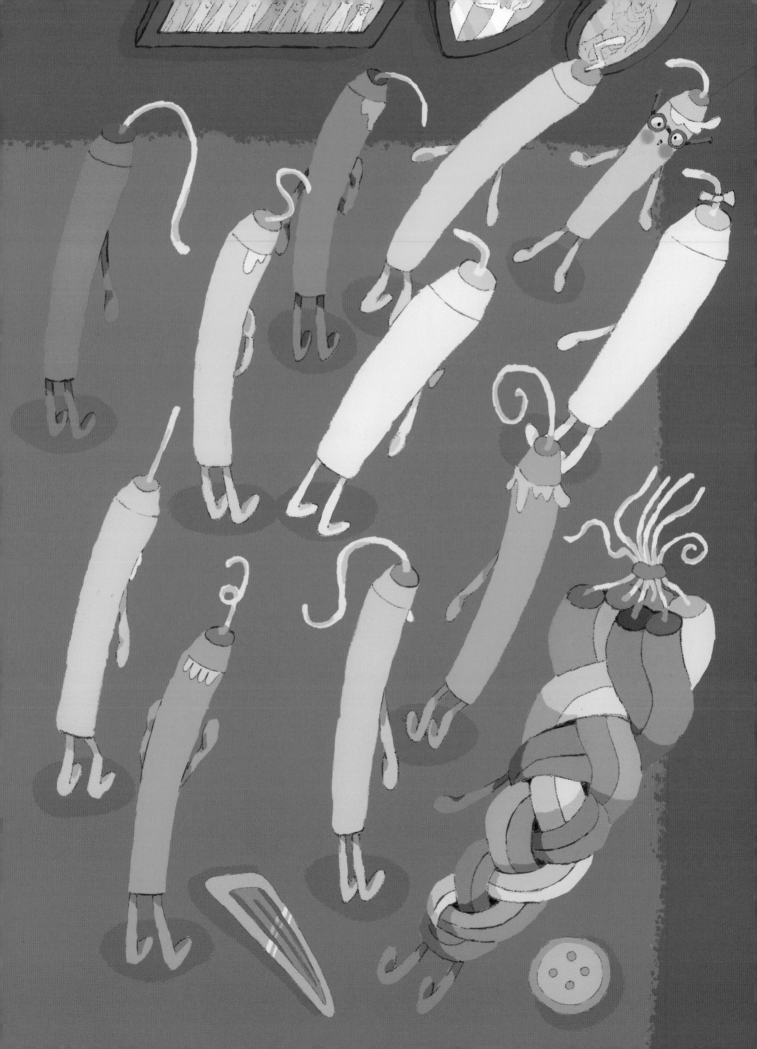

"You are absolutely correct, Little Flicker," Waxy said. "Maybe you should be the first night's candle."

"Oh no," he quickly responded. "There are plenty of better candles than me, like Sparky and Sparkle or Ms. Wicks. Smokey is older, and Blaze's flames are brighter. Twinkle and Glow burn so beautifully. Really anyone is better than me," he insisted.

"Yeah," the candles exclaimed. "Pick me!" one called out again. "No me!" another yelled. Waxy thought about it for a second. Maybe Little Flicker was right. Maybe I should find someone else to be Hanukkah's first night's candle. But I also need a candle to be my helper.

"I need a helper, a *shamash*," Waxy explained. "I need a special candle to help me light all the other candles. Little Flicker, you think about others first. You support the other candles. You encourage them to go ahead of you. So I need you, Little Flicker, to help me too—to be my helper candle," Waxy decided.

There was a gasp in the drawer. The candles looked at each other, embarrassed. They were so worried about who was going to be the first night's candle, they hadn't even thought about helping each other. Little Flicker, whose flames barely glistened, should be the *shamash*, the helper candle.

All the candles were silent as the drawer opened wide. They heard a voice say, "Let's get our *shamash* candle."

As if they were one, all the candles pushed Little Flicker forward. They wanted Little Flicker to be on the highest place of the menorah.

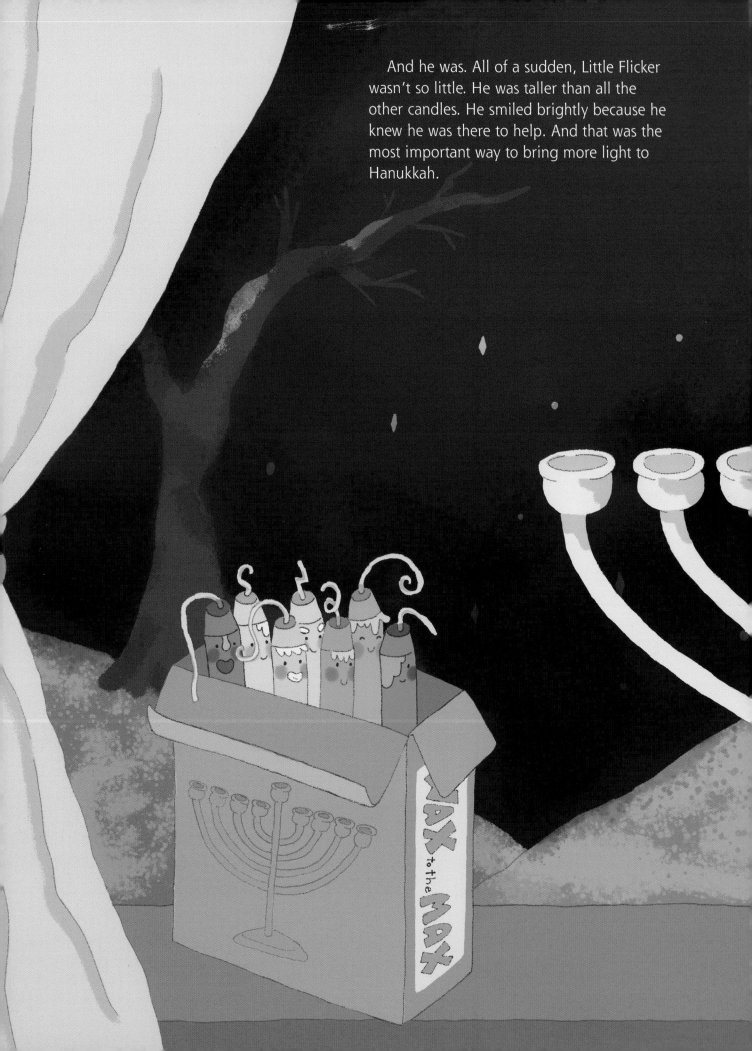

And he was. All of a sudden, Little Flicker wasn't so little. He was taller than all the other candles. He smiled brightly because he knew he was there to help. And that was the most important way to bring more light to Hanukkah.